A KISS FROM A DEMON

KISS FROM A MONSTER SERIES
BOOK 1

CHARLOTTE SWAN

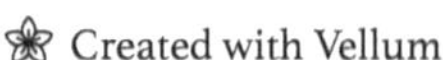 Created with Vellum

TROPES & CW/TW

Tropes & Kinks: Breeding Kink, Degradation Kink, Praise Kink, Virgin, Monster Romance, Extra-Long Tongue, Double Penetration, Size Difference, Bondage, Spitting, Mild Blood Play

CW/TW: Dubcon, sexual harassment (not between MCs), Violence, Gore, Predatory behavior by an adult towards a minor (mentioned, not between MCs)

This book is dedicated to everyone who's wanted to fuck a monster. If that isn't you, turn back now…

1

IRYS

I t is desperation that sends me out into *The Woods* tonight.

A desperation laced with fear that has me walking into this cursed land as the sky above fades from warm gold to poisoned black. It is as if the sky is warning me to turn back. To stick with the demon I already know and find a way to defeat it with a more conventional method.

I am all ears if the sky could tell me how I get out of marrying Duke Brayborne.

However, I suspect it would offer the same advice everyone else in our village has: to grin and bear it. To be happy in the knowledge that, while my husband may be old and cruel, at least I will have a home. I will have food in my belly this winter and I will eventually have his children. That is the only true joy a woman can look forward to in her life. By becoming a vessel to produce heirs and enjoying their love until they are old enough to leave home and start their own families. Continuing this whole hideous cycle again for a new generation.

Well, I want no part of it. If making a bargain with the

demon they say dwells in this forest is the only way to save myself then I will take that risk. Why must I suffer for my father's mistakes? All of my older sisters were married off to men at least close to their age. Men that they may not love but at least have respect for. Duke Brayborne has lusted after me for as long as I can remember. It is remarkable I was able to avoid him and reach my twenty-second birthday.

Unfortunately, my luck had run out. With the Duke in attendance at my birthday dinner, my stomach sank as my father announced that I was to marry him. My father, Lord Evergrove, has an affinity for drunk card games. An addiction that led him to gamble away all his tenants' money. Duke Brayborne was willing to overlook the debt if my father gave me to him as his wife.

A trade my father contemplated on for a few moments until Duke Brayborne threw in a keg of ale and one-hundred gold pieces. That is all I was worth to my father. Ale and some gold he gambled away within the hour. When my mother died on my seventh birthday he began to sink deeper into himself. He never cared whether I came or went, and refused to have a tutor brought in to see to my education so he could spend more gold on his drink. When the townsfolk began remarking on my beauty as I grew he saw an opportunity. Especially when Duke Brayborne was the one who began showing the most interest in me.

I shudder and shake myself from that train of thought. No point in dwelling on my misfortunes, I will get the life I deserve no matter what it costs. Anything is better than being the wife of that horrid man.

The sun has fully set now and the moon has taken its place high in the sky. Its pale light and the soft glow from my lantern are the only things guiding me through *The Woods*. Shrouded in myth and mystery, no one dares spend enough time in here to create a map of its layout. I only know about the creatures in this forest thanks to a healer woman who goes into these parts to find the herbs that will not grow in town.

When I confided my plight to her she took pity on me and informed me that something in these woods helps desperate humans for a price. I am hopeless enough to believe she is telling the truth.

I do not have much money. Only a few gold pieces I was able to hide away when my father wasn't looking. I can only pray that it is enough.

The healer said to head in from the north side of *The Woods* and walk until I reach a house with a twelve-pointed star on the door. She said that if I felt like I was getting lost, I was on the right path. Which is not very helpful seeing as how I have felt lost the moment I crossed under the first mangled oak tree.

The snow and ice that has covered our village does not dare go into these woods. My long, brown cloak snags on branches from the gnarled trees above. The boots I am wearing are a size too small and I can already feel a blister forming on my heel as I sidestep thick roots bursting through the forest floor like vengeful fingers. A wind blows through *The Woods*, rustling the leaves and tugging at my braided back dark hair. It holds a bite that makes my cheeks sting. The scent of dank earth overwhelms my senses.

I keep walking, listening for anything that may tell me I'm on the right path. Even with its lack of snow, the forest is colder than our village. The dangerous magic that permeates the air has me pulling my cloak tighter around myself. Passing by another tree I swear I have already walked by, the breeze picks up again. Only this time it seems to push me in a new direction. I'm so desperate for anything to guide me that I let myself be led by whatever invisible force this is.

After a few moments on this path I see it.

For a moment, I doubt myself and wonder if it is too late to turn back. This cabin, if it can even be called that, is built into the base of a massive hill. Roots make up the thatch roof and curl their way around the door like veins. Obsidian stones chart a path up to the dark wood door that is marred with the marking the healer mentioned. There is an odd scent in the air and a soft glow peeks out from beneath the door.

Something is definitely home.

Perhaps this was a trick? Maybe the healer woman has a deal with this creature to lure unsuspecting young women to its door to devour them. If that's the case then I might as well meet my end. If it won't eat me, something definitely will if I try to find my way back to town.

I hesitate for another moment as I look up at the door. I remember Brayborne's wrinkled face and stale breath as he whispered in my ear how he's been waiting to bed me since his wife died. His wife...who had passed just over ten years ago.

Swallowing down the bile in my throat I march towards the door and knock once.

The sound echoes into the cabin beyond. I wait for a sound; I wait for something to stir behind the door. Half expecting it to be ripped from the hinges and me to be picked up by a monster and swallowed whole but nothing happens. I knock again, the old, wooden door soft against my knuckles. It is rotted through enough that, coupled with the rusted latch, it swings open.

I do not know if demons have the same type of manners we do but I can imagine they wouldn't take kindly to someone walking uninvited into their home. Left with no other choice, I do just that. As soon as I cross the threshold I know I have made a mistake. The heavy door slams shut behind me and it feels like I'll never get the chance to walk out of it again.

Even as the temperature inside the cabin warms my bones I know I have to keep on my guard. I set my lantern down on a small wooden table by the door and take in my surroundings. The cabin is...nice. There are tools scattered along what seems to be a workbench. The kitchen is sparse with a few pots and pans hanging from the walls. The wooden floor is maintained and the rugs are clean. A few potted plants and books for herb cataloging sit along a counter that faces a small glass window. A lingering scent of stewed meat wafts through the air.

This cabin feels otherworldly. A tingle forms at the base of my neck as I take a step deeper into the cabin. It is so quiet in here, the only noise coming from my breathing. It's enough to make me believe I am alone. Until I see him.

How had I missed him before?

I gasp and my heart beats faster. He stands in front of a roaring fireplace. A massive figure that almost entirely blocks the flickering flames from my eyes. Dressed in a heavy, wool cloak he turns towards me. His massive horns are gnarled like the branches of the trees outside, almost brushing the high ceiling of the cabin. The fire behind him illuminates his ghastly features.

His face is a skull made of weathered gray bones. The only sign of life are the flames from the fire pouring into his eye sockets to illuminate him from within. The room seems to glow even brighter and my feet are carrying me closer to him despite my fear. There is something else I am feeling as

I get a better look at him. Something I have never experienced before.

It started out as fear tightening my belly but it is some other emotion tickling it now. Maybe it is the powerful form and just how unknown his kind is to me. That unknown feeling has traveled lower, to my most feminine flesh and heated it. My body is rebelling from the warnings my brain is issuing.

The figure turns fully towards me now, his expression unreadable. Though I suspect it is hard for a skull to emote.

"Who are you?" He asks, his voice is deep and skates over my skin making me clench my teeth and thighs together. I should not tell him my name. The healer woman warned me against it but for some reason I cannot recall why.

"Irys Evergrove." The answer spills from my lips. Well, so much for keeping secrets. The demon tilts his head as if assessing this answer to see if I am lying. He hasn't tried to eat me yet so I take that to mean I should press on with my demands. "I have come to make a bargain with the demon of *The Woods.*"

A sound rasps out of him and I think he is laughing.

"I do not make deals with little girls." He waves a clawed hand, dismissing me.

"I am not a little girl. I am a woman of twenty-two. One who is being forced to marry a hideous man in the morning if I do not find some way to stop it. I've come to bargain with you to stop my marriage."

I take a deep breath unsure why I feel compelled to say the next bit.

What is wrong with sharing the deepest desire of my heart if I am already bargaining with a demon?

"I wish to bargain for the chance to marry someone I truly love."

The cabin has grown hotter. My palms are beginning to sweat and I wipe them on the soft material of my cloak. Those fiery sockets track the movement without saying anything. They linger on my hands before traveling up the length of my stomach, to my chest, and then to my face. It is not in the same manner in which the Duke looks at me and maybe that is the reason more wet heat has found its way into my most intimate parts.

"And what did you bring to bargain with?" I reach into my satchel under my cloak and dig around before my fingers close over the crushed velvet pouch. Pulling it from my bag, I hold the purse out toward him. My meager ten gold pieces barely jingle as he extends his hand and the purse floats towards him on an invisible breeze.

His claws sift through the bag counting each coin. Shame makes me hang my head and look at the toe of my boots. I count the scuffs on the wooden floor until I hear him laugh again. The sound curls my toes and I know the tips of my ears are pink.

"I have no interest in the gold of men. Especially not this...*humble* amount."

Shame floods me. Even a demon will not help me escape my fate. I truly am doomed to endure that horrible cycle that took my own mother from me. Forced to pass this curse on to my own children. No, this cannot be it. I will find another way.

I have to find another way.

"Thank you, demon. I'll see myself out." Turning to leave his voice booms behind me.

"There is something else you can offer me." He extends

the clawed hand holding my purse toward me. "Something I find much more valuable than a small bag of coins."

I furrow my brows in confusion. "I have nothing else. You hold in your hand all of my worldly possessions."

"That is not true. You possess something much more precious than gold."

His gaze rakes down my body again, devouring it with that eyeless stare, and then it clicks. No, surely this demon cannot mean...But did not the healer woman warn me? He may ask for something more than money. I never thought it would be that.

My sisters always said I was too gullible and I would pay the price for it one day.

"I am not bargaining with that. If I wished to be defiled for my first time I would stick with the Duke," I spit. Even as the words leave me I cannot help but feel that I am wrong to categorize these two in the same way. Would it be defilement with this creature?

Why does it feel like I would enjoy it?

The demon bares his teeth in a feral grin. Each one is pointed and razor sharp as he takes a thunderous step towards me. The wooden boards groan under his massive frame until he is only a few feet away from me. I have to crane my neck all the way up to be able to look at him in those flame-filled eyes.

"Defile? I would give you pleasure no mortal would ever be able to, little human. I would have you shaking around my cock, begging for my seed, while my tongue fucked your ass." My breath hitches at his vulgar words. Those are the types of words I have only heard my sisters whisper. They're coarse...*dirty* and yet the flesh between my thighs grows even damper. Why did I like to hear that? Surely this demon wields a power to make me desire this profanity.

"If you agree to lie with me tonight, to give me your maidenhead, I will agree to your bargain. That you will only be able to marry someone you truly love." He leans down even closer to me, his warm breath smells like pine trees and sends a tingle down my spine.

One night. All he is asking is one night of my life and I will be able to get what I want. Perhaps I do not marry the man of my dreams as a virgin but it is a small price to pay to be able to marry him at all. If I let this monster have me tonight, hopefully these odd feelings I am having towards him will be satiated. My curiosity will be fulfilled and I will be able to live out my life in a marriage of my choosing.

There is one thing I have to ask before making my decision.

"How would that even work? How would we even"—I swallow—"fit together?" The demon chuckles and the fireplace flares behind his frame. A breeze kicks up and makes his cloak swirl around him. One moment I am looking up at a flaming skull the next, a pair of black eyes are peering down at me. Long, dark hair tangles in the horns on his head and has two sharply pointed ears sticking out from the mass of it. Skin of the palest gray and lips peel back to reveal normal teeth aside from two extra sharp fangs. He is still massive but he has shrunk by at least a foot.

This figure is more human but no less monstrous.

"Better?" He asks, his voice softer too. There is that dark part of me that preferred his rougher tone.

I shake my head and I can feel a blush warming my cheeks. This will be the man—the creature—to whom I will give myself to. Who I will lie with of my own choosing if that is what I wish. Do I wish for this? As if he read my mind, my demon speaks.

"Do we have an agreement?" He holds out a clawed

hand for me to take. An ominous offering that will bind my fate to his tonight.

One night. Just one night. I repeat that to myself as I stare at his hand. *Think of all you are gaining for just one night.*

"We have an agreement," I say, clasping his hand. I watch as he traces his clawed thumb over the back of my palm. Even as I repeat to myself this is only one night, something tells me that that will not be the case.

2

ASGORATH

I t has been a millennium since a human has interested me and found its way to my door.

However, none of them have ever intrigued me as much as this Irys does. Normally humans beg me for the same mortal requests: eternal life, unending wealth, and undying love. Pathetic, really. Those things can be so easily taken away. They are normally so desperate and self-absorbed that they do not even realize they have bargained over their soul to me in the process.

Alas, that is all a part of the job. You cannot get everything your heart desires without paying a price. A price I have never wanted anyone to pay more than Irys. For some reason, I entered into this bargain with her without one of my failsafe curses. Something I use to make sure that no matter how powerful the humans I work with figure themselves to be, I am the one who gets the last laugh. They will toil in service to me for all of eternity.

My desire for Irys has me wanting her to serve me in a different way.

It is truly unfortunate that the only human I have

wanted to keep in my whole existence is the one who bargained with me for her freedom. I cannot put my finger on why I want her so much. Maybe it is those green eyes of hers that would give even the most bloodthirsty creature pause before feasting on her flesh. Maybe it is those full lips that I am desperate to see wrapped around my cock. Or maybe, just maybe, it is because she is the first human to come to me and not be repulsed by my form.

Irys fears me, to be sure, but I excite her as well. Does she think that I cannot smell how wet her cunt grows in my presence? That her sweet scent has not been tempting me since she walked through the door? Men and women, old and young come to bargain and each one of them are disgusted by me. I taste it on their scents even as they beg me to pity them. Their condemnation of who I am seeps from every pore.

They do not look at me with thinly veiled lust like Irys does.

Knowing that she is still in possession of her virtue, I had to be the one to claim it. Before some other mortal got to her, my treasure. My Irys. Convincing her with pretty words that he loved her only so he could take what belongs to me. I will give her pleasure no mortal man could ever live up to.

She will be begging me to keep her once I get my cock inside her.

Looking at her now as she stands before me, her small hand still pressed in mine, there is an innocence about her that goes beyond her sexual inexperience. A shyness. That makes my heart, something so shriveled and worn out I am surprised it still works, beats faster. It demands I claim her, keep her, kill for her so she never wishes to leave. To protect her from the darkness of the world and keep her safe in my cabin for eternity.

We have a long night ahead of us and while she may desire me, it is clear she does not know why. Her thighs will welcome me when that part of the night comes, for now, I need to work on gaining her trust. In the morning, I will worry about making her mine.

Reluctantly I drop her hand and she uses it to grip the side of her cloak.

"So...what now?" she asks in a timid voice. Time to test her limits.

"Where do you want me to take you first?" Her green eyes widen and pink stains her cheeks. Her hand trembles where it grips her cloak even as her arousal turns her scent sweeter. My poor little human. Who taught her to be ashamed of these urges? Soon she will give in to her desires. She will see there is nothing to be afraid of when I am the one who has the honor of pleasuring her.

"I—I don't know. The bed, I guess? That's where my sisters did it." The soft timber of her voice makes my cock harden. I would love to capture the sound and bottle it. It would be something I would bargain away all of my power to keep.

"We have all night," I say softly, reaching out to run one of my claws along her soft cheek. Her answering shiver has me biting my tongue before I rethink my idea to take this slow. "A creature like me wants to take his time savoring his prize."

My claws reach for the tie of her cloak. Her hands fly up as if to stop me but they pause mid-air as I undo the delicate bow. The brown cloak falls open leaving her in a light blue gown. It is made of a sturdy, cotton material but the hem and stitching are fraying. When she is mine I will have her draped in the finest silks, encrust her in the finest jewels mortals are so eager to part with in return for some selfish wish.

I would not part from Irys for all the jewels and gold in the world.

"Pretty girl," I growl and she shyly looks down at her boots

Reaching behind her, she stiffens before my claws find the thin leather band holding her braided hair back. With one gentle tug, the long, dark strands are freed. My fingers itch to embed themselves in it. For my claws to prick her scalp and to wind the length of it around my fist, snatching her head back while I pound into her from behind.

Patience. She robs me of all of it.

"Have you ever been kissed, little human?" I ask and her answering blush tells me all I need to know even before she shakes her head. This pleases me greatly. I will reward her for this with my tongue later.

"Are you hungry?" Her stomach growls at my question. She needs her strength for what I have planned. I grasp her by her upper arm, even as she struggles in my grip, and steer her toward the old, oak dining table. Her slight resistance only hardens my cock further in my pants.

Irys sits at one side of my table and I sit on the other. My cloak drapes down to my feet and I brush my hand over the dust collected on the table's surface. I cannot recall the last time I sat and had a meal here. Irys and I will dine here every night going forward.

With a wave of my hand, a wide array of food appears. Steaming bowls of broth filled with all types of vegetables. Roasted meats drenched in rich sauces and paired with mashed potatoes. Even a three-layer cake sits at the far end, decorated in pink and yellow icing. There is a goblet of wine for each of us but not enough to make her drunk. I want... no, I need Irys to remember everything that happens tonight.

To remember why she should stay with me.

"I've never seen this much food," Irys mumbles, half dazed as I spoon a portion of everything on her plate. My claws clink on the dish as I set it down in front of her. I watch as she picks up the metal fork I forged and begins to dive in. As much as I love her eating the food I prepared for her, my teeth bare at the fact that she has not been taken care of.

Mistaking my displeasure as being directed towards her, she sets her fork down and wipes her mouth, tucking a strand of dark hair behind her delicate ear.

"I apologize, where are my manners? It's just been so long since I've been served this much. The winter has been hard for us all. Even with my father being the lord we've only had a few plates of food between the two of us. Though I guess that has more to do with—" She stops talking and looks down, twisting her hands in her lap.

"More to do with what, Irys?" I am eager to know more —anything—about her.

"Nothing, I shouldn't have said anything. I should be grateful my father has kept a roof over my head all these years." She picks up her fork again but she is eating slower, more measured. "My father is a good man, deep down. He just lost his way."

"You are starving," I say. "Your father let you starve."

"It's more complicated than that," she says, but I see the shock in her eyes. Uncertainty coloring her features as she considers what I've said. "Isn't it? I honestly don't know anymore. I was taught to be grateful. That so many people have it worse than me. My father said he was the only one to have my best interests at heart but then he marries me off to the Duke for…" She trails off again, the color leaching from her face.

"Tell me, Irys, how did this marriage come to be? A marriage you felt so trapped by you sought me out." Without her pathetic excuse for a father, Irys and I may have never met. That is the only thing I will be ever grateful to him for.

It still may not be enough to spare his life should his path cross with mine.

"My father gambles and he owes the Duke money." The truth comes pouring out of her like someone uncorking a barrel of wine. "The Duke has been after me since I was a child. Always staring at me, always following me when he wasn't supposed to. He never touched me, even though I could see that he wanted to. I thought I had avoided him. That surely some nice man from the village would catch my eye and marry me before the Duke had the chance to."

My teeth clench at the mention of her desiring other men but I do not interrupt. Irys clearly needs to share.

"I should've known something was wrong when the Duke attended my birthday dinner a few nights ago. How my father proclaimed that we would wed in one week's time. I can still feel the Duke's hand on my arm as he told me how long he's been desiring me. How it was only a matter of time before my drunkard father toiled away too much coin and it was up to me to help my father by performing the duties of a wife."

Her voice is soft and I see the tears shining in those wonderful eyes of hers. The Duke will be dead, even if the bargain did not necessarily hinge on his death, I will make it so just for scaring her this way.

She laughs but it holds no humor.

"Ale and some gold pieces are all it took for the Duke to secure my hand. No matter how much I begged and pleaded, my father wouldn't hear of it. The truth is, he never had much time for any of his daughters. Our mother took on that responsibility alone and when she passed, and all my sisters were grown and out of the house, there was no one left to raise me. No one has ever cared much about what happens to me. No one has ever wanted to keep me for me." Her green eyes find mine and they are so sincere. "The Duke wants me for my beauty, he does not want me."

"Then he is a fool. And the only good fool is a dead fool." Irys rears back her eyes wide.

"What do you—"

"Eat your dinner, Irys. You have a long night ahead of you." I drop my fork before picking up a leg of chicken and ripping through it with my claws. "Besides, you already walked into my cabin uninvited. Proper manners have no place in a demon's dwelling."

Irys smiles shyly at me and that may be where my obsession with her turns into love.

Regardless, pride blooms in my chest as I watch her tuck into her meal with gusto. She eats spoonful after spoonful, polishes off a massive piece of chocolate cake, and finishes her wine. In the warm light of the fire, I watch her eyes grow heavy and soon her head lays against the back of the chair.

I could stare and watch her like this for the rest of my days but, I do not want her to injure that lovely neck of hers. Scooping her up I marvel at how small she is. No matter how hard I wish to fuck her I have to remember to exercise a bit of restraint, lest I risk bruising this unblemished skin. Irys does not stir as I carry her deeper into my home.

She barely makes a sound as I make my way into the bedroom and lay her down on the dark sheets. Rolling over onto her side I watch as my massive bed cocoons around her. Waving my claws, the fireplace is set ablaze. Irys is about to spend a considerable amount of time naked and I will not have her cold.

I stand over her, marveling at her one last time. She needs her rest, to regain her strength for what will be a night she will never forget.

3

IRYS

I want to stay wrapped in this delicious warmth forever. My father has not had the money for firewood in weeks so this is a real treat. Usually, I go to sleep bundled in at least three layers. When did he get the money for this? A gift from the Duke?

That thought has me shooting up as I take in my surroundings. I am in an unfamiliar place. An ornately carved fireplace is on my right illuminating a room I have never been in before. I am tangled in dark sheets that are so soft I imagine this is what sleeping on a cloud would be like. Especially when I am in this massive mattress that is high off the ground, with over a dozen pillows decorating it.

I am not in my father's home.

The intensity of the fire seems to double and suddenly I am being suffocated. I rip off my thick gown and toss it aside, my socks and boots follow shortly after that. Dressed only in my shift I can finally breathe deeply. The fire licks along the bare skin of my arms and then I remember.

The Woods. The demon. Our bargain.

He let me sleep after dinner? The demon seemed so

singularly focused earlier. With a shaking hand, I feel my way down my body. Slowly taking into account everything until I reach the apex of my thighs. I do not feel as though anything about me is different.

My flesh down there is damp and I know it is not all from sweat. As my own hand grazes up my inner thighs I let out a soft moan. Everything seems to be in order. That is at least a small relief.

Laughter echoes from the corner of the room and I gasp, nearly jumping out of my skin.

"Believe me, little human, I want you wide awake when I claim your maidenhead. To hear the scream you make when my cock enters your unused, little hole."

He rises from a chair placed against the far wall. How long has he been watching me? The demon moves slowly, his horns dragging along the low ceiling as his cloak opens to reveal a hint of his muscular torso. Gray lips are pulled back into a predatory smile as he advances toward me, stopping at the foot of the massive bed.

"Wait," I say and his dark eyes survey me. "I don't even know your name."

Shame makes me drop my eyes. I am going to let this demon inside of me and I did not even ask for his name.

"Asgorath."

"Asgorath," I repeat back and his nostrils flare as a shiver wracks his body.

"You'll be moaning it soon enough." Asgorath unbelts his cloak and it drops away revealing pale gray skin stretched over a heavily muscled body. His upper arms bulge with every movement, and his powerful thighs are clad only in dark pants. There are markings that decorate his stomach and chest. Intricate symbols I have never seen before.

Another reminder that my first time is not going to be with a human.

I watch with uneven breath as he kneels upon the bed and makes his way toward me. Apprehension has me slipping back towards the headboard. That only makes him chuckle, the sound damping my flesh even more.

"Did you put something in the food?" I ask. "Why does my body respond to you like this?"

His horns glow in the firelight, reaching towards me like hands.

"You already agreed to give yourself to me. I have no need to rely on the tricks of man to make you willing," he says. I know he is right. There is something about Asgorath that makes me feel safe. Like at dinner, somehow telling him all of that stuff made me feel lighter. Made me feel like I finally had someone who cared enough about me to listen.

That realization sends another batch of moisture slicking out of me. Asgorath inhales deeply and wraps a clawed hand around my ankle. He pulls me gently so I slip down the bed, laying fully on my back in the center of the massive mattress. I squirm but it is of no use, his strong hands are there pinning my arms to the bed.

"Are you ashamed at how wet you grow for me? For the beast that will rut you—fuck you as your virgin blood runs down my cock—until you are a quivering mess?" His voice has grown deeper, more gravely. "You should be disgusted with yourself. Shouldn't you?"

Asgorath's claws pull my arms over my head as he crawls on top of my body. His hard muscles press into my breasts and I cannot help but moan. I have never been touched like this, never been this close to anyone or anything before. Unkissed and untouched and my first ones will be claimed by this demon.

He rocks against me gently, something hard presses into my damp center and my hands strain, seeking anything to hold on to.

"I am a creature so feared and reviled, but your pussy gets wet all the same. A disgusting creature holding you down makes you drip down your thighs. Admit it."

I shake my head but that only causes more of the hardness to rub against me. It feels so good I need more. This need is so potent I am writhing underneath him, trying anything to get more friction. His teeth coast down my neck.

"Use your words," he teases, pullings his lower half away from me and that wonderful hardness is gone. My whines reach my own ears and it is clear all logical thought has left me. I am solely focused on the pleasure that he was giving me. I care about nothing else but getting it back.

I will say anything, even though what he is asking me to admit to is the truth.

"Yes. Yes!" I yell, lifting my hips to try and get him to press back against me.

"Your pussy gets wet for a monster. Say it." I shake my head, I am not that far gone. I do not use language like that. I never have.

"Say it, and I'll let you rub your greedy cunt all over my cock until you come." Asgorath's hips drop down just slightly and I feel him against my center again. My pussy, he called it. Pressing against me once, twice until I am shaking. Only for him to pull away from me again. Tears of desperation sting my eyes and I thrash again in his grip.

"My pu...pussy gets wet for a monster," I bite out and I am instantly rewarded. His hips slam back against me and then he is moving. Slamming our lower halves together as his teeth nip at my skin. His dark hair tangles with my own, getting caught in my sweat and tickling my face. I am obsessed with his woodsy scent which has gotten even deeper since he crawled into bed with me.

My legs rest on either side of his hips and my shift rides up. Dangerously close to baring me completely but I am too lost to care. He continues his movements, the seam of his pants and that hard bulge behind it keep grinding against me. The pleasure builds in my stomach, and my thighs begin to shake but Asgorath keeps going.

"I'll keep your secret," he says into my neck. I can feel his muscles constricting with each thrust against me. "No one from your village knows that you're the demon's pretty little whore. Begging to rub your clit on his cock. Dry-fucking me for all you're worth."

The words are my undoing. My muscles seize and I feel new moisture leak from my pussy and course down my thighs. My eyes bore into his as he looms above me. A thin layer of sweat covers his forehead and I do not know what expression is on my face. All I know is that I lean up to capture his mouth and suddenly my body is no longer coming down.

It is flaring back to life.

As if in shock it takes my demon a minute to realize his mouth is on mine but he does. Asgorath's tongue tangles with my own. My inexperience is clearly showing but he does not seem to care in the slightest. The flavor of his mouth is wonderful, so crisp and delicious I want to drink it down. His growls rumble through me as he lets go of my wrists to spear his hands in my hair. My own hands find their way to his back and dig into the corded muscle, eliciting a deep groan.

I will do anything to get that sound out of him again.

We come up for air and I think that the kissing portion may be over but once I have sucked down a few breaths

Asgorath is back. His tongue invades my mouth only to slip in deep, passing my own tongue until I feel him tickle the back of my throat. My eyes fly open but he continues. Sliding his tongue farther down until I choke, my eyes watering.

"That's good to know," he says softly. Before I get the chance to ask what he means or how he did that with his tongue, his hands leave my hair and tangle in the top part of my shift. With one harsh tug, Asgorath rips it clean down the center, baring my naked body to his eyes.

When I was still covered my shyness had been kept at bay. In the heat of the moment, when pleasure had been my sole motivation my brain temporarily forgot where we were and who we were with. It all comes flooding back to me now and I make to cover myself.

That was the wrong move.

Asgorath growls and pulls my arms away from where they went to shield my naked breasts.

"Never hide this body from me." He uses his magic to pin my arms to my sides and I squirm. This is when the apprehension creeps in. I do not know if I am ready for the full thing yet. Panic starts to turn my breathing ragged. As if he can read it on my face, Asgorath leans down and places a soft kiss on my lips. "Relax, my little human. You came so hard on my pants I need to see it. Need to lick it all up and drink down your pleasure."

He kisses me softly again before nipping at my bottom lip. "When it's time for me to put my cock in you, you'll be begging for it."

Asgorath moves down my body, peppering kisses along my neck and throat. Stopping to swirl his tongue around my left nipple while he rolls the other one between his claws. Pinching and twisting it so that my back arches off the bed.

The pain only heightens my pleasure. His sharp teeth scrape over the first nipple before he switches to the other. As he comes away from them, I see the pale pink buds slick with his saliva.

He lifts his head and gazes into my eyes. My chest is rising and falling; I try to free my arms again but it is futile. Without breaking eye contact I watch as his jaw drops open. Lower than any man's jaw ever could. Then slowly, I watch his tongue unfurl. Dark red and forked, wet with saliva that drips onto my stomach in soft splashes. He drags that long tongue around each of my breasts, squeezing them as he goes while licking my nipple.

I gasp, my hands pulling at the sheets. There is a euphoria unlocking in me. A heady sense of belonging and righteousness as I watch his tongue trace down my stomach, leaving behind a trail of spit. No man would ever be able to give me what I know he is about to. They simply do not have the motivation or the equipment to.

When I stopped being unsure of Asgorath seeing me naked I do not know. But whenever it was, my body has already decided that here and now, we belong to him.

I will worry about what that means in the morning, as far as my future is concerned.

If I thought him licking my breasts was amazing, when his tongue laps over my pussy I feel like I am going to bust out of my skin. His eyes are still locked on mine as his tongue drags over the top of my pussy, taking a moment to circle around a bundle of nerves that has my toes curling, before licking through my folds. I can hear how wet I am, the sloppy sounds his tongue makes as he licks up my first climax all the while preparing me for my next one.

My eyelids become heavy as the sensation becomes too

much. My sisters have definitely never mentioned their husbands ever doing this to them.

Asgorath growls and his tongue pulls away from my wet flesh, curling it back into his mouth. My eyes fly open and I let out a whimper, wanting more of his attention, wanting to reach that peak that only he has ever brought me to. Magic releases my hands and he slides down my body, kissing below my navel, the top of my pussy, before looking up at me between my legs.

My thighs rest on either side of his cheeks, and his horns loop up toward me.

"Oh, Irys. Only naughty little girls have pussies this wet." He licks up my center and my hands fly to his horns to keep him there. "Sweeter than anything. It's a wonder you've kept this cunt untouched. You knew it belonged to me, didn't you?"

I nod my head. "Yes, yes. Please keep licking me."

"Beg me to eat your pussy. Beg me like the greedy slut you are." His tongue licks me again and I scream in frustration. I need it. If I do not get it I am going to die.

"Eat my pussy, please. It's yours!"

He attacks my pussy with renewed vigor. He rubs his nose against that sensitive bundle and laps at me over and over. I am not prepared for what it feels like when his tongue enters me. The overwhelming sense of fullness as he pushes past my entrance has me jerking on the bed. His clawed hands lock under my thighs and press them up and back towards my body, baring me fully to his mouth.

I grip his horns harder and I'm afraid I might break them. My screams echo off the cabin walls as I feel his tongue expand wider inside of me. Asgorath licks along the barrier of my maidenhead and I try to squeeze his head with my thighs. His tongue retreats and he looks up at me. His mouth and chin are wet from my arousal.

"Going to be such a tight fuck. You're going to be my pretty, human plaything. Even if this is wrong, your little pussy wouldn't listen. Isn't that right?"

"Yes, it needs you! I need you, please." The words slip from my lips but they are true. I need him, in this moment and perhaps even beyond it. He has unlocked something inside of me. Something I will never be able to hide away with shame again.

The wet, messy sounds my pussy makes as he continues his work help propel my body into climax. He rubs his face all through my wetness before sucking on that bundle of nerves again. My thighs squeeze him even tighter than before. He does not stop, does not once come up for air until my release barrels into me. The breath is knocked out of me and I scream his name. My back has arched clean off the bed and I feel like I am weightless.

Floating forever until I am able to reenter my body.

Asgorath gives me one final lick that causes me to shutter before kissing his way back up my body. My mind is fogged with lust but I know one thing to be true. I do not fear this demon. No man would be so thorough in my pleasure, would not even know how to give me this. Asgorath is also letting me set the pace. He knew I was not ready and gave me pleasure all the same, instead of demanding I open my legs so he could find his own release.

I do not know if I am ready for him to be inside me like that yet, but I do want to show him I appreciate what he did. More than that, I want to be able to give him the pleasure he just gave me.

He will just have to teach me how to do it.

Reaching my face he presses a soft kiss to my lips and I can taste myself on him. Even after coming so hard, I feel myself grow wet again. His long tongue licks up my cheek and I smile up at him, letting my hand trail down his muscled stomach. I stop at the waistband of his pants and look into his dark eyes.

"May I lick you?"

4

ASGORATH

I f this human was not already mine, that soft question out of her mouth sealed her fate.

May I lick you?

My cock is the only one that will ever feel the soft, wet cavern of her mouth. To push all the way down her throat until she is choking, tears leaking from her beautiful eyes. I tested her gag reflex earlier and she should be able to get me down a good distance. I will push her, though. Her limits are mine alone to test.

"You want to put your virgin mouth on my cock?" I ask and I love watching her blush. That same delicate pink matches her nipples and the soft skin of her knees. Her pussy is red and swollen from my efforts. Begging for more of my attention as my gaze lingers on it.

"Yes," she says, eyes bright.

"Do you think I should allow you to do that? Have you earned the right to service my cock?" Her breathing picks up and her breasts rise and fall faster.

"I want to give you pleasure like you gave me." She swallows. "I want you to teach me how to pleasure you."

"Will you let me come inside that pretty mouth of yours? Will you swallow it down like a good girl even if you're choking?"

She nods, her eyes straying down to the top of my pants. Irys moves slowly, trailing unsure fingers down past the waistband. Her slender fingers undo the simple lacing and they sag around my hips. Dipping her hand inside, I growl loud enough to shake the bed.

Her small fist rubs my cock and stars shoot off behind my eyes. Gripping my own pants. I rip them off and bring my cock into view. Irys's hand flies to her mouth and she scrambles back, no doubt wondering how she is going to accomplish the task she has set out to complete.

My cock sticks out from my body, already seeking the warm, tightness of her cunt. It points at her like an accusation. In this form, it resembles more of a human male's cock. The head and shaft are smooth, and decorated with only a few dark veins. A bead of my come already sits at the tip and I hear her gasp as more rushes out in front of her eyes. Warm, stickiness slipping down the side of my shaft and dripping onto the sheets.

"Do not be scared, little one. My cock will only give you pleasure, even when you are not sure you can take it." I wrap my hands around her ankles and pull her down the bed, her dark hair fanning out behind her. "Now get on your knees."

Dropping Irys to the floor, the fire from the hearth illuminates her in a warm glow. She sits back on her heels looking up at me. Her full lips are open and she runs her tongue along the bottom one. I stand above her, jerking my cock in my clawed hand over her face. This act is deliciously crude. She is an angel I am about to sully for my own pleasure.

An angel who I can see dripping onto the carpet.

I sit on the edge of the bed and spread my thighs. Waving a clawed hand, I motion her forwards. Irys crawls towards me, that ass of hers swaying with each movement. Damning myself for not tasting that hole earlier, I make a mental note to explore it later.

"Look at how you tremble. My greedy cock whore wants to taste her demon's dick. To drink his seed until it fills her belly," I say and her moan in response is all the confirmation I need. "Kiss it, little one. Kiss it how you kissed my mouth, we will go from there."

Irys slides closer until her mouth is level with my lap. Her small hand replaces mine around my shaft. I watch her hesitate for only a moment before her pink lips kiss the crown of my cock. My come already there coats her lips and I growl as she licks it off. As she tastes me her eyes grow more unfocused, the sound of her arousal hitting the carpet is music to my ears.

Kissing the tip again I watch her grow bolder. Tentatively slipping her pink tongue out to run along one vein and caption more of my spend to drink down. She moves her fist up and down and my balls hit against my inner thighs. Irys discovers them at the same time and runs that curious tongue along them as well.

"Do...do I only kiss you here?" Another perfect blush. "You did more than just kiss my pussy."

"I licked you until you creamed all over my face. Lick my cock, feast on it my beautiful slut, and I'll treat your face to the same reward." Irys loves how I speak to her. I felt it when I was growling those same words against her pussy, being rewarded by more of her delicious juices.

A growl rips from my chest as she flattens her tongue and licks the underside of my cock. Over and over again she tastes each side of my cock, coating them in her spit. She licks at my tip and is rewarded with more of my seed that she drinks down. Licking lower she runs her tongue along each ball before returning to my shaft.

"Such a hungry little girl. You were starved for food but more importantly, you were starved for cock. Don't worry, I'll make sure you get your fill of each every night."

Moaning around the tip of my cock, her eyes connect with mine once more. The flush of her cheeks, her wild expression, and the saliva running down the corner of her lips is beautiful.

Irys smiles at me as she opens wide and takes me fully into her mouth.

I pitch forward on the edge of the bed which causes my cock to go deeper into her throat. Gagging slightly, she does not stop. The muscles of her mouth work in tandem with her hand, sucking and tugging me until my vision blurs.

"My perfect little cock-slut. You were born to suck cock." I growl as she takes me deeper, watching tears leak from her eyes. "Only my cock. Mine. No man will ever get to see you like this."

Her nod is frantic as she continues to work me. Never stopping, only more and more eager to taste me. My self-control is in short supply. My claws tangle in the soft strands of her hair and grip her skull. I want to get deeper, but she is so small I do not know if she is ready for that.

Irys's hand squeezes my knee and she nods her head. She knows what I want to do and she is giving me permission. *Mine.* I will brand her name on my skin.

Gripping her head even tighter, I release myself. I bring my hips up to meet her mouth as I drive her face down into my lap. My cock not only bumps the back of her throat but goes down it. She swallows and the pressure makes my teeth grind. She does not protest, she does not stop me.

Irys holds on to my knees and lets me face-fuck her for all that she is worth.

The sounds from her mouth are wet and obscene. I feel her nose bump up against my stomach and my toes curl. I slam her down harder, not sure how much longer I can last.

"You're perfect, my perfect little toy. I said I wouldn't defile you but that's exactly what I'm doing." Irys lets out a moan and then chokes around my length again. Her tears land on my thighs, the salty smell of them an aphrodisiac to me. I feel myself start to spray more come into her mouth that she greedily drinks down until she is gagging again.

Her nails dig into my knees and I know she is at her limit. My brave little human.

I rip her off my cock and she tries to catch her breath. Those green eyes are bloodshot and wet, her mouth is smeared with a mixture of her spit and my seed. Those plush lips are bright red and swollen. I should have come down her throat but my possessiveness demands I claim her in a more primal way.

After all, I did promise to come on her face like she came on mine.

"Sit back on your knees and open your mouth." Irys does so immediately. "Good girl."

My clawed hand moves in a frenzy as I tug on it over her face. Her breathing is turning ragged again, her nipples are pebbling under my stare and I watch a stream of wetness coasts down her parted thighs.

"Please give me your come, Asgorath. Please reward me with it."

Her soft voice saying my name is all it takes. I let out a bellow that has the birds nested in the ceiling scattering off. The first rope of my come lands on her tongue, before sliding down her chin. The next ones land lower on her chest, dripping down on her breasts. I come and come and come until her mouth and chin are painted in my release. The white, sticky substance clings to her skin and her dark hair. My scent mingles with hers.

My chest moves with labored breaths as I watch Irys run a finger through the seed on her collarbone. She lifts that finger to her mouth before swallowing it, licking the extra from her lips. What a picture she makes. Covered in my come and dripping her own.

"Thank you," she says. "Did I please you enough to let me suck your cock again?"

I growl and scoop her off the floor.

"You'll be sucking my cock every day for the rest of your life." Irys giggles before nuzzling into my neck. Stickiness coats me but I do not mind it. I am just grateful that I have her in my arms, so trusting and content.

I will keep her this way for eternity.

With a wave of my hand the antique copper tub turns on and hot water fills the basin. Grabbing a handful of herbs and salts I throw them into the water until it is cloudy and emitting a woodsy scent. Irys is still in my arms, watching me from half-closed eyes. Once the bath is full the water switches off and I lower both of us into the warm water.

Irys lets out a soft moan and stretches her legs out in front of her. My cock is wedged between the cheeks of her ass and I grit my teeth. I wash her gently, cleaning away my spend, secure in the knowledge that I will be covering her in more of it in the coming hours. Scrubbing her scalp she sighs and tilts her neck to give me better access. The silence between us is comfortable. A comfort that I am already attached to.

"Asgorath," Irys says softly. I hum as I reach for a basin

of fresh water to rinse the soap from her hair. "You know I do not have much experience...with any of this."

I nod, setting the basin down and reaching for a towel to keep her clean hair out of the dirty water.

"My sisters always said I was gullible and it would get me in trouble but, I don't have anyone else to ask."

"Ask me, little one. I'll tell you whatever you wish to know." I feel her take a deep breath.

"Is this normal? The way I feel towards you? My sisters respect their husbands but they never have spoken of this... desire. This need to be pleasured is all I can think about. I can't imagine them feeling this way and being able to keep it quiet."

My heart thunders in my chest. My little human desires me. Irys wants me to pleasure her and can think of nothing else. This warms me and my claws slip down her sides, dragging along her smooth skin, before coming to rest on her hips.

"Your sisters are not married to men who could give them this. No mortal man can give you this." My claws slip lower until they part her folds eliciting another sweet moan. "Your pussy recognizes this. Your heart does too. It understands and desires to be kept by me even when your brain still believes it wants a normal man. You've never truly wanted a human man and you never will."

I slip a claw just into her entrance and she throws her head back against my shoulder. She is ready for me. Finally.

"Now it's time for me to prove it to you."

5

IRYS

Asgorath dries me with a plush towel before leading me back into the bedroom.

I do not know when he became so handsome to me but he is. I love the way his dark hair tickles my sensitive skin. Love the way his claws tease me and pinch my nipples.

But most of all I love how much he wants me.

Call it wrong, given what he is and how we met, but I am beginning to realize that maybe I want him to keep me. I do believe him when he says no man could ever satisfy me and it is evident to me that I can never live without this pleasure. Sometime between when he was licking my pussy to me sucking on his cock I made the decision that I would remain here in the morning.

To see what life could be like with him.

As someone who grew up unwanted and passed around, his possessiveness over me makes my hunger for him grow. No one has ever wanted me. My sisters abandoned me to start their own lives, my father used me as a bargaining piece but Asgorath...

Asgorath could have demanded I stay with him. Could have put that into the bargain and I would have had to agree but he did not. He told me he would give me pleasure and then I could do as I wanted. To marry who I wanted.

Is it wrong that I can no longer see that person being anyone other than him?

Perhaps I should desire freedom. To be able to start a life where I am able to pick and choose what I want and where I want to go. But hasn't Asgorath given me that? Would he keep me locked in this cabin? Would I even want to leave?

These are all things I will grapple with in the morning. Right now I will sink into this deep pool of lust and give myself fully to my demon.

Walking into the bedroom I see that the sheets have been changed. Unlike the dark ones before, these are bright white, tightly tucked into the mattress. I look up at Asgorath with a raised brow. He sets me down gently, leaving me covered only in the towel.

"I want the proof that I was your first time. Your virgin blood will soak these sheets and I will keep them as my most treasured possession." My answering blush makes me dip my head. I look at the soft bed and drop my covering. The wet strands of my hair tickle my back as I crawl onto it face first.

My first time. I should be as nervous as I was at the start of the night but I am not. This is the right time. This is who I want and who I know will take care of my needs. I am not afraid, I am ready to give myself to him.

The *real* him.

Asgorath makes a move to join me but I sit up.

"I want you to take me in your true form. The one that I first saw you in." Shock has his dark eyes widening.

"Are you sure? That form can be even more...demanding

than this one." I nod my head and he steps back from the bed. With a deep breath, he begins to transform. His body glows with a warm light pulsing, shimmering and shaking as it reveals his true form. His skin begins to tear to reveal black hands the color of the night sky that tapers down into deadly sharp claws. With a few groans and snaps, his horns lengthen and become even more gnarled. The skin of his face peels back, ripping through bone and flesh until a skull is all that's left behind. The fire from the hearth is pulled through the air. It threads itself through one dark eye socket until his gray skull is lit from within.

"It seems my greedy little human demands more from her demon lover." He runs that extra-long tongue over his sharp teeth. My pussy starts to drip and I watch him inhale the scent. "Be warned, little one. My other form had a bit more control. I cannot promise that when I am like this I will be able to be gentle."

In this form, he towers over the bed. At least another foot taller than he was before and wider too. His cock is definitely larger, I can barely make it out in the firelight but I know it will be even more magnificent. My thighs rub together and those fiery eyes track the movement. I should be scared, should change my mind and have him switch back to that more palatable form. However, I do not ask for that. Instead, I crawl forward on my hands and knees and grasp one of his clawed hands, falling on my back and pulling him down on top of me.

"However you fuck me will be right. I want you to ruin me for anyone else." Kissing a skull is a new sensation. There is no give and it feels like I am kissing a warm, smooth stone. I do not care though. Not as my tongue glides under those sharp teeth to pet his. His growl shakes the bed, the air turning thick with desire.

"My seed has made you bold, little human. Let me give you more of it."

"Please," I whine. "I miss your taste."

His cock stretches between us, rubbing up and down my stomach, already seeking to enter me. My earlier suspicions were confirmed when I feel its size. It spans the length from my hips to my breasts. As well as it being adorned with ridges along his shaft and tip. How will those feel inside of me? My thighs squeeze at the question and I know I cannot wait any longer to find out.

I push up on my heels to try and align him to my entrance, but his clawed hand wraps around my jaw and forces me to look at him.

"Once I am inside you and I have your blood running down my cock, that is it for you. I will own you. Your cunt, your body, your heart. It will belong to me. Should you try and run from me..." His deep voice grows rough, coasting over my skin and turning my nipples hard. "I'll find you and keep you locked in this bedroom for all of eternity."

"Please, I want to be kept." The truth tumbles from me before I have a chance to suck the words back in.

"You better mean that, Irys. Besides, I can't have my little fucktoy wandering too far, someone might try and take her from me." His hand moves from my jaw down to my throat. "And I do mean try, for if anyone succeeded I'd kill them with my bare hands."

The violence, the vulgar words, it is too much for me to bear.

"Please, Asgorath, I need you inside me. I can't wait any longer."

"Oh Irys, we haven't even begun and already you're a soaking, pathetic mess." His clawed hand leaves my throat and trails down the center of my body. He stops briefly to tug at my nipples, scraping his sharp teeth over each of them. His hand goes lower, over my pussy before cupping my folds. I moan and grind myself against his palm.

Lust has taken over and I need him more than I need my next breath.

"Wet and soft. That's how you'll always be in my presence. Wet and waiting for me to pound this tight pussy." Asgorath gives my feminine flesh another squeeze and my eyes roll to the back of my head. His tongue extends from his mouth, licking up my chest and leaving behind a trail of moisture.

"Please, Asgorath."

"You need me to fuck this cunt?"

"Yes!" I scream. "Please."

"I told you you'd beg me," he laughs, his claws slowly sinking into my entrance. "Now let me get this little, pink pussy ready to take this demon cock."

With one finger inside of me, the pressure is almost too much. When he adds a second one I almost come clean off the mattress. His fingers are thick, and those dangerous claws scrape softly inside me, not too far as to break my maidenhead but enough to have my toes curling. Unfurling his jaw once more, that long tongue slips out as it licks a path down to where his fingers are parting me.

"Your greedy little clit is begging for my attention and it's too sweet for me to ignore." His magic lifts my legs, tilting my hips so I am completely exposed to his face. My fingers grip the white sheets as his tongue laps at that bundle of nerves, my clit, and works it over and over in tandem with his claws. He fucks me with his fingers, while his tongue makes love to the rest of me.

"I wonder if this hole is just as sweet."

His tongue pushes against my back entrance and I

scream. My skin breaks out in a hot rash as I thrash on the bed, trying to break out of his hold. *Not there, oh my... anywhere else but there.*

"Embarrassed? You shouldn't be. As my whore you will give me entrance into all your holes whenever I want to use them. Whether it's for my pleasure or to give you yours." He smirks even as his tongue presses harder against my forbidden entrance. "Maybe I'll fuck your ass tonight as well to rid you of this shame."

"Please...d—d—don't, not there!" I thrash as his tongue pushes past the tight ring of muscle. Those fingers of his have not stopped pumping into me but the added fullness of his tongue makes my muscles strain. It's too much, way too much. Tears leak from my eyes. The pleasure barreling into me will break me. Snap me in half and I am scared of it.

The fear is what propels me forward.

Asgorath's tongue pushes in deeper, his fingers tickle the walls of my pussy and I start shaking.

"Come on my fingers, greedy girl. Come while my tongue is stuffed in your pretty little asshole." As if I can do anything but obey. My thighs shake and squeeze his head, my knuckles turning white where they grip the sheet. Perspiration breaks out of my skin as my climax hits me. A fresh wave of my come coats his hand and he growls. My stomach is in knots as my muscles continue to lock.

It takes me a moment to regain control of my breathing. It takes me another moment to realize Asgorath has removed his fingers and is pushing the tip of his cock into my entrance. My muscles are relaxed and my thighs are still held in place by his magic. He bares down on me as he feeds me one magnificent inch at a time. The fire in his eyes rages. Whatever emotion he is feeling it is a strong one.

The first shallow thrust is pleasant. The second one is

filled with pressure. On the third one, I feel him break through my virginity, I look down to see the red drops sink into the sheets. Asgorath's tongue sneaks out to lick over another nipple again.

"You belong to me now, your purpose in life is to serve me in this bed."

My brain is fogged and I absentmindedly realize he is not even halfway inside me and it already feels like I am being split in half.

"My purpose is to serve you." Another inch of his cock fills me, those ridges making my head fall back on the bed. "Forever."

"Even if it hurts?" he asks and I nod. He grits his teeth and leans down to meld his mouth to mine. "Forgive me, little one. This is the only pain I'll ever cause you."

That is the only warning I get before he jerks forward, burying himself completely inside of me.

The scream I let out is inhuman. I buck underneath him to try and move away from him and the pressure he's caused inside of me. There is pain, but he does not try and move. His fire-filled eyes bore into me as his clawed hand wraps around my throat.

"Hold still. Hold still. The pain will be over soon, let yourself adjust."

His hard mouth rains kisses all over my cheeks and mouth. The longer we stay still the more the pain begins to subside. Those ridges inside of him caused me discomfort but now I need to know what they feel like as he thrusts inside of me.

"This naughty pussy couldn't resist me for long. It needs a good pounding and that's what I'm going to give it." His mouth returns to mine and his hips retreat before slowly pushing back in.

The sensation is everything. I am so incredibly full I could burst. I feel his warm tongue slip into my mouth and it keeps pace with his thrusts. His wonderful pine scent fills my lungs and I want to be consumed by it. The hard skin of his body rubs against my nipples and it only adds more to the pleasure.

"Tiny and tight. If I wasn't already from Hell, fucking your cunt like this would surely damn me there for eternity." Picking up the pace, his hips rear back and slam into me. The muscles of my ass jiggle with the impact as the sound of our bodies slapping together only increases my arousal. I can hear the wet slurping sounds my pussy is making as he pounds into me.

His tongue creeps deeper into my mouth, past my teeth, and tickles the back of it. I gag and cough around it but that only spurs him on further. Licking up the back of my throat tears blur my vision as he increases his brutal fucking. My breasts bounce in time with the impact.

"Open your mouth," he says, pulling his tongue from my throat. I obey without question parting my lips and sticking out my tongue. His face looms over me as his tongue hangs out, grazing my own. I watch as a trail of saliva slides down it and into my waiting mouth. So much pours from him and I can feel it slip down my throat and spill out over my lips.

"Swallow," he commands and I all too happily obliged. He spits down, another patch of saliva lands on my lips that he promptly rubs in with his clawed hand. It's vile and disgusting to be degraded in this way, but I crave it all the same.

He sees it in my eyes and his mouth widens into a grin exposing those sharp teeth.

"Dirty, little human. Letting me defile her virgin cunt with my demon cock. Watching her swallow down my seed and my spit. You're a vessel for my pleasure, that's all you'll ever be."

"Yes, please. I want more of your come."

"Inside of you, little one?" he asks. "Inside this pretty pussy."

"Yes, inside of me. Anywhere!" I scream. His pace hasn't slowed down. The force with which his hips slam against mine leads me to believe I'll be bruised in the morning. Bruises I'll be wearing with pride.

"I'm going to fill you up. My come will flood your tiny cunt."

Taking both my wrist in one clawed hand he pins them down above my head. My body is taut on the bed and can do nothing but absorb his rough fucking. The posters of the bed creak and groan with each of his thrusts as the headboard smacks against the wall. He leans down to lick up my neck before nipping at it with his teeth. My muscles are cranking tighter and tighter. My hips tilt as much as they can to get him even deeper. His ridges press against a secret spot inside of me and my nails dig into his hand.

"Clenching down on me so you can receive my come. This greedy pussy will be drowning in my seed." He slams into me once, twice, and on the third time, my climax hits me. "Take it. Take every last drop, good girl."

My screams echo around us and mingle with his groan. I feel his warm come shoot into me over and over again. True to his promise he floods me. The hot liquid slips out around where we are joined and joins my blood on the sheets. Asgorath still pushes into me even as his cock softens, the squelching sound makes my cheeks heat.

As he continues to fill me I am struck by how right this feels. Everything about this moment is perfect.

"Asgorath," I say, my voice hoarse from screaming.

"Thank you. That was beyond anything I could've imagined."

"Was?" he chuckles. "Oh, little one, we are not done yet."

Before I can react, his strong forearm is wrapped around my middle and flips me onto my hands and knees. His claws snag at my hips and he pulls my ass up toward his face.

"Did you really think I was only going to have one round with this pretty cunt?" He runs a claw through my folds and I watch as he sucks our mingling releases into his mouth.

"But our bargain—"

"Said you would give me your virginity and that you would spend the night with me. The sun is not rising anytime soon." Asgorath squeezes one of the cheeks of my ass. "And I will be inside each one of your holes tonight."

I don't get the chance to protest before I feel him pushing into me again.

"You should see the mess I made in your pussy. My seed makes sliding into you so much easier. Your only purpose is to take my come, isn't it?"

"Yes, Asgorath," I say, my ass tipping up toward him. Reaching down he winds the length of my hair around his fist, making my spine curve even more and my eyes look up at the wood beams of the ceiling.

"Did you mean it?" I choke out as he continues slamming into me from behind. My arms feel like mush but I support myself, absorbing each brutal impact.

"Mean what, greedy girl?"

"That you're keeping me?" All movement stops and the bed quits its creaking. Shame makes me stay quiet. I should not have asked. Perhaps this is what all lovers say in the heat of the moment and in the morning light both parties part ways.

If he rejects me now, in this state, I will never recover

from the embarrassment. From the vulnerability I am showing him in this moment.

His chest comes down on top of my back and I feel it shake with laughter. Is he laughing at me? Heat presses against my closed eyes.

"See what happens when someone tries to take you from me," he whispers in my ear. "Then you'll know if I mean it or not."

Asgorath's warm breath tickles my cheek as I feel his tongue lick down my back. Tasting the sweat that lingers on my spine until slipping through my parted ass cheeks.

He said he would claim both holes tonight. He said he would keep me. Asgorath is a demon that keeps his end of the bargain.

That wet tongue pushes through my back entrance, stretching me until my muscles burn. It goes deeper than before. With Asgorath fully sheathed inside of me, I've never experienced being this full. This pleasure is not meant for this world, it is not meant for humankind.

But I have tasted it and I will never live without it again.

"Only naughty whores question their master." He drops my hair and pushes my chest down towards the bed. "Cheek to the mattress while I fuck those doubts out of you."

My demon does just that.

6

IRYS

S oft sunlight filters into my eyes, waking me from the deepest sleep of my life.

Groaning, I bury myself under my pillow, stretching out my legs beneath the sheets. It is tempting to believe I dreamed Asgorath up. The story is certainly absurd enough. A woman wandering into *The Woods* in order to escape her marriage. Only to be pleasured by a demon who wants to keep her forever.

If it was not for the soreness between my legs I may have believed that it was all just a figment of my imagination.

Disentangling from my sheets I wake up to find that I am alone in this massive bed. I could not tell you how many times Asgorath buried himself inside of me, but by the final time, I could barely keep my eyes open. My demon pulled himself from me despite my hissing from the lack of connection and gathered me to his side, careful not to impale me with his horns.

The whole night I slept safe and wanted in his arms. Arms I want to be in again right now.

I swing my feet over the side of the bed and stand. All at

once a rush of his comes leaks out of me and drips down my thighs. Smiling, I take a tentative step toward the bathroom, gritting my teeth at the discomfort. I need a pain reliever herb, the healer woman told me those are the ones she comes into *The Woods* to find. If those plant cataloging supplies were anything to go by, I am sure some is grown around here.

Wetting a towel with warm water I gently wipe away the blood and stickiness from my thighs. I find a stack of clean clothes laid out for me. Ones made of much finer material than the ones I arrived in. Making my way upstairs I wonder where Asgorath is.

The cottage is quiet and I can smell fresh bread baking. He probably just stepped out for a moment. Collecting my cloak I fasten it around myself before pushing through the door and standing in the front lawn. *The Woods* are still dangerous but in the morning rays they are not quite so ominous.

Or maybe that is because I have Asgorath to protect me now. Perhaps *The Woods* are just welcoming me as their new inhabitant.

A quick survey of the yard and I find the bright blue leaves of the plant I am looking for. There is only enough for two cups of tea but that should be all I need to soothe this ache. I smile, realizing I should probably plan to collect some extra to have on hand.

Pulling it from the ground I go to put it in my satchel when I hear it.

Gallops from horses. I stand there frozen until they come into view. My heart beats wildly and I cannot register what I am seeing. No, it cannot be.

My father and the Duke are here. They have come to collect me.

Both sit atop white stallions, flanked by two soldiers on their opposite sides. My father's eyes are bloodshot and his skin is greenish in color. His normal look after a night where he found himself particularly deep in his cups. While my father is battling a hangover, the Duke looks livid. His wrinkled skin is red and his eyes pierce right through me.

My skin crawls at the reminder that I was supposed to marry him today.

Not anymore though, Asgorath saved me from that. He gave me my freedom back and I am using it to choose to stay with him. With that newfound resolve, I square my shoulders and face both men.

"Lady Evergrove," Duke Brayborne calls out. "Your presence is required in town. Did you think *The Woods* would keep you from fulfilling our marriage arrangement?"

"I do not have to marry you." My father seems to be coming out of his stupor and slides down from his horse.

"Daughter, why have you dishonored me? I gave you to Duke Brayborne to wife and you fled? If we hadn't gotten it out of that healer woman where you might be, we may never have found you." My lord father walks closer to me and I back up a step. "You're coming home to be married. Running away from your duty is unbecoming of a woman your age. You are lucky the Duke still wishes for your hand after you dishonored him."

Where is Asgorath? Surely he would not allow them to take me.

"I do not have to marry him, father. I made a bargain with the demon in these woods."

"And what, pray tell, did you offer this creature, daughter? You have no money to tempt him with."

Heat rises to my cheeks but I refuse to feel shame over what Asgorath and I did.

"Myself." Father rears back as if he has been struck, shock contorts his features. The Duke lets out a deep laugh and shakes his head, his beady eyes narrowing with disgust.

"Foolish girl!" My father makes a grab for me but I jump back out of his reach.

"Selling yourself to that beast will not save you from me." The Duke dismounts from his horse, the last three strands of white hair he has blowing in the wind. His yellowed teeth bare in a grin at me. "I will delight in punishing you for your desertion, you traitorous whore."

Dropping my satchel I look around. *Asgorath please show yourself and make good on your half of the bargain.* Both the Duke and my father advance on me. I could make it back into the cottage but they may catch me in there and drag me out. I was never very quick at climbing trees either.

A gentle wind tugs at my hair, the same wind that propelled me to Asgorath's door in the first place. It pushes me to *The Woods* behind the cottage as if urging me to run as fast as I can. That is when I remember Asgorath's words from the night before.

Should you try to run...I'll find you.

I have to believe he was serious in his threat. Without a moment to lose, I turn from my father and the Duke and sprint deeper into the heart of *The Woods*. I hear the Duke shout something behind me but I am already moving too fast. The breeze is pushing me as I pump my arms and legs. My cloak and hair snag on the branches as my feet jump over the uneven ground. I keep going, willing Asgorath to realize something is wrong and save me.

The sound of hooves hitting the ground pound in time with my heart.

There is a break in the trees up ahead and I know I just

have to make it there. I keep going, even as I feel them closing in on me.

"Get back here, Irys. I'll wring your neck once I get my hands on you." The Duke's threat sends a chill of fear down my spine and makes me run even faster. My heart is racing and my legs are throbbing from the effort.

I burst through the clearing and that is when I see him.

Still, in his demon form, his cloak drawn tight around himself. In his hands I see a large bushel, the telltale blue leaves of the pain reliever plant. Relief and happiness make my steps falter and tears rush to my eyes. The glow in his eye sockets sparks.

"Were you trying to run from me, little one?" He calls across the clearing just as I hear the gallops close in on me. His head snaps to look behind me and without giving him an answer I run straight toward him until my arms are wrapped tightly around him.

"Don't let them take me, please. Don't let them take me back." I sob into his chest, relishing his warmth and strength. "He still wants to marry me, Asgorath. He'll kill me if I go back, please don't let him!"

The thunderous sound of hooves has stopped and I hear a loud gasp behind me. Opening my eyes I look over my shoulder to see all of the men frozen in fear. Even the Duke has paled and he reaches for the sword at his side, brandishing it Asgorath. The two other soldiers follow suit

Asgorath is unruffled by them. Waving a clawed hand I watch as the Duke's sword is yanked from his grasp. Asgorath flicks his wrist and the blade spins in time with his hand, flying high above the Duke's head until it stops with the blade pointing down.

"This is for tainting her scent with fear." It is the only warning my demon gives before the sword drops, impaling the Duke. Crimson blood leaks off the tip of the blade as it protrudes down his chest. With a meaty thud, he hits the forest floor.

The soldiers in the Duke's employ meet a similar fate.

My father's eyes are as round as teacups as he takes in the gore. He looks up at me, at how I am grasping this demon like he is my lifeline. Father shakes himself and then drops to his knees. He clasps his hands in front of him and raises them towards me.

"My daughter, my beautiful Irys. I have been a terrible father to you. Letting that lecherous duke anywhere near you was my fault. I am sorry. I am so sorry for how you have suffered in my care." His green eyes, the same color as mine, beseech me. "Spare my life and come home with me. Away from that creature and you have my word that you can marry whoever you want."

Asgorath stiffens next to me. Does he think I would so easily leave him? Silly demon, he is mine for all eternity as well. I wrap my arms tighter around his middle.

"I am sorry too, father, but my bargain states I can only marry someone I love." I tilt my face up towards my demon, his fire-filled eyes warming my face. "And I've already found that."

A clawed hand cups my cheek and tilts my head up before hard lips caress mine. I break the kiss needing to end this once and for all. To sever all ties to my old life.

"I will have my demon spare your life if you agree to tell everyone in the village I ran away. That the Duke and his men tried to find me but met with an unfortunate accident. You will promise to never come and look for me again. You will tell no one what has happened to me." My father is already nodding his head. "Do you agree?"

"Yes, yes please just spare me."

My eyes meet Asgorath's and he nods.

"Be gone father, the daughter you knew died in *The Woods* last night. Who I am now is someone else."

Without so much as a backward glance, my father scrambles to his feet. Quickly mounting one of the white stallions he turns on his tail and gallops out of the clearing.

He always was pathetic. I realize that now.

There is a stretch of silence before Asgorath breaks it.

"Did you mean it?" he asks. I nuzzle my face into his chest, inhaling his earthly scent.

"Of course I meant it. I'm waiting for you to say it back." My face heats and I shake my head. "Unless of course, you don't. Which is fine. I don't know why I expected you—"

"Irys, what I feel for you is stronger than love. It is an obsession. One that will completely consume me if I let it." His claws tangle in my hair and gently scratch my scalp. "I'll live every day for you. For your pleasure."

His mouth descends on mine and I moan into our kiss. That wonderful tongue of his tickles mine. Leaving my hair, his claws tangle in the tie of my cloak, undoing the bow and letting it pool at my feet.

"Well then, don't let me keep you from your life's purpose." Reaching behind me I undo the laces to my gown, letting it drop and join my cloak at my feet. I stand there under his fiery stare completely naked. He lets loose a growl before taking one of my breasts in his hands.

"Should we enter into another bargain?" Asgorath asks, licking my nipple until I squirm.

"What did you have in mind?"

"That you'll spend all eternity telling me how much you love me...and I'll spend an eternity showing you how much I love you." I bark out a laugh. Gripping the sides of his cloak I pull until he too is gloriously naked. Dropping to my knees I take his magnificent cock in my hand, roughly pumping him twice. Licking up the come that has already beaded at the tip.

"This may be the second easiest bargain I've ever agreed to," I say, before taking his cock all the way down my throat.

EPILOGUE
ASGORATH 5 YEARS LATER

he Woods have never felt more like my home than they have in the past few years.

I always viewed this realm as a part of my job. A job that has experienced an uptick in customers recently. I guess the story of a young woman finding her way into the path of a demon who bargained to get the life of her dreams will do wonders for business. My purpose in this land is to fulfill bargains and gain more power.

But it does not truly satisfy me like Irys does. Nothing ever will.

Once this latest bargain is done I can get back to her. Already my mouth waters for a taste of her sweet skin. Over the last five years, my desire for her has only increased. I need to be inside her every moment of the day. If there were no bargains to make or food to prepare I sometimes think I would never pull out of her. Living out the rest of eternity in the warmth of her pussy.

Speaking of bargains, I watch as the elderly fisherman in front of me hands over his bag of saltwater pearls. The last of his late wife's possessions so that I will grant him his favor. I shake the bag in my clawed hand. His red hair is graying around the sides and his face is weathered by a life spent at sea.

"Your offering pleases me. In exchange for these pearls, I will grant you luck on the high seas. That your catches will be bountiful. You will be the envy of every other sailor in your company."

He gives a surprised gasp and clasps his hands.

"Thank you, thank you. It is for me and my daughter. She is only sixteen. This is to keep her fed."

I grunt at him ready for this exchange to be done. Besides, this fisherman is a fool and will soon have to face the wrath of Kraken of the Darksea. A fate he should have taken into consideration before coming to me.

"Your reasons are your own. Our business is done here."

Tucking the pearls into my cloak I let my magic wash over me and suddenly I am at the door of my cottage. Our cottage. A life the two of us have built. No more cold, solitary nights when she is with me. We spend countless hours a day getting lost in each other. I've taken her on every surface of this home and it is still not enough. It will never be enough.

Irys has blossomed in the short time she has been with me. After her father departed it became apparent to me that he did not think to give her an education. She was embarrassed by her lack of ability to read or write when I asked her to help me catalog some of the plants that grow around the cottage. I kissed away her embarrassment and made it my goal to teach her everything. True to my word I have.

From the history of the world to how she can take me in her ass for hours on end. She has become the best pupil any teacher could hope for.

I wonder what Irys is up to now. Studying? Cataloging some more of the wildlife? Pushing through the door, she is not immediately in front of me and that displeases me. Normally, when I return from a bargain she can't wait to get her hands on me.

The bag of pearls is removed from my satchel and I study it. I had planned on giving it as a gift to Irys but the more I think about it, surely it is bad luck to give your own wife the pearls of another man's dead one. I set them at the table by the door and call out to my obsession.

"Irys?"

"Down here." Her soft voice reaches me and my cock instantly hardens.

My Irys wants to play. I know she is in our bedroom and I quickly shed my humanoid form. After all these years, Irys still prefers my true face. It makes her so wet I only use my other form when I am making a bargain.

My feet stomp through the house until I am outside our bedroom. There she is, my beautiful wife. Lying on our bed completely naked. Her dark hair is fanned out around her and her delicate wrists are bound to the headboard by a thin scrap of ribbon. A soft, shy smile on her full mouth.

Instantly I am salivating over her. I shed my cloak so I am just as naked as her and I watch her rub those smooth thighs together. Circling around the bed I drag one of my claws up the center of her body, swirling around each nipple, before slipping it into her parted mouth. She moans as she sucks on my finger, with the same vigor she gives my cock.

Leaning down I whisper in her ear.

"You know I love you?" I ask.

"Yes," she says around my finger, continuing to take it deeper into her mouth.

"Good because for the next few hours"—I rip my finger from her mouth and use my thumb to keep it open—"I am going to fuck you like I don't. Like you are nothing more than a naughty human slut who wandered into the demon's lair."

My jaw unlocks and I watch as my tongue licks over her chest and through the dusting of dark hair on her pussy. I watch her eyes go glassy as she pulls against the restraints when my tongue finds her slick folds. Delicious. I lick and lick until sweat breaks out along her forehead.

Pushing my tongue into her entrance, I lick along her walls until I butt up against her womb. She moans, her thighs squeezing against my ears.

"Such a beautiful whore. You'll let me put my tongue in your ass as punishment, yes?" I ask. She was shy about it in the beginning but she loves her ass being fucked now.

"Y—yes," she stutters out.

"Won't be much of a punishment, will it? Naughty girls like you like having their two holes stretched at once, don't they?" Her head nods vigorously. My tongue coasts lower until it meets her little asshole. It takes nothing for my tongue to slip in now, though she is still as tight as the day I first claimed it.

I push my claws into her, scissoring both fingers and stretching her tight pussy while my tongue fills her ass. Irys moans my name and begs me in an incoherent voice until I feel her cunt clamp down over my fingers. She soaks my palm, her come shooting out of her and drenching the sheets below.

Pulling my tongue out of her, I eagerly lap up her moisture before crawling up the bed to straddle her lovely face. I am careful not to rest my weight on her as I push my cock into her warm wet mouth. In this position, she cannot take me as long but she sure tries.

"Cock-hungry slut, aren't you? You suck me so good, little one. You want to earn my come."

"I do," she garbles around my length. My hands grip the headboard for leverage as I slam myself down her tight throat. Irys chokes, her nose and eyes leaking to mix with some of my come already spread on her face. The bed creaks under the force of my thrusts as I drill her face into the pillow. It is obscene what I am doing to this beautiful creature but she craves it just as much as I do.

Feeling my spine tingle I pull myself from her mouth and stroke my cock in front of her face. She keeps her eyes open as her lips part and she sticks out her waiting tongue. My come lands with a splat on her chest, painting her breasts in my release. I spread some of it along her lips before pushing the tip back into her mouth.

"There you go. Good girl for cleaning up my cock like that."

Her green eyes are dazed but she smiles at me, preening under my praise. As much as she loves being my greedy, little whore, she loves being my good girl just as much.

Reaching up I untie her wrists before sliding down her body. Gripping her hips I flip her on her hands and knees. I fold her arms behind her back before tying them so that her shoulders are the only thing supporting her upper half on the bed.

At this angle, both her holes are presented so nicely to me. Asking me which one I would like to fuck this evening. With Irys, I never have to choose.

I have been waiting on showing her this surprise but it feels right to give it to her now. My tongue licks a path up her spine, before dipping once into her ass and once into her pussy. I spit on her pink asshole and watch as it drips into her already wet folds.

"Irys?"

"Yes?"

"Will you let this monster take both your holes at once?" I ask, gripping one pale ass cheek.

"You know I love your tongue in my ass," she whispers, as if she is still shy to admit that.

"Not my tongue this time, little one. I've been working on a surprise for you." My magic zips through me and I can feel myself take on the transformation. I watch as my lower half glows faintly and then it sprouts out. A second cock, identical to my first one, only placed a little higher.

Gripping her hips I press both cocks to each of her respective holes.

Irys lets out a moan and writhes on the bed. Powerless to do anything while I have her immobilized.

"Asgorath...what is—how?" she asks, already leaking even more moisture from her pretty pussy, coating the head of my cock nudging her there.

"My girl loves my cock so much I had to give her a second one. So that I can fuck both her ass and pussy at the same time. Thank me for giving you what you need." Irys moans and tries to push back. My clawed hand smacks her ass, leaving behind a bright red handprint. I spank her again, digging my claws in to heighten the sting.

"Thank you, thank you!" she babbles.

Without warning, I plunge both cocks inside her. The feeling is incredible. She grips me so tightly in her cunt and ass that it is like having two fists wrapped around the most sensitive part of me. I pull back gently and can feel the twin ridges on my cock rub each other through the thin barrier that separates her ass from her pussy.

"Asgorath, it's too much! I can't—"

"You can take it. You were made to take my pounding. That is the only thing you are good for." Irys lets out another shriek as I retreat farther out of her before slamming all the way back in. This is some of the roughest fucking I have ever given her. It may be too much.

Just as I think that I watch her push back to meet my thrusts. Her breathing comes in pants not from fear but from arousal. She wants this. My greedy girl just needs to be fucked by me. It is what she always needs.

"I don't know if two cocks will be enough to satisfy you. There's still one hole left open." My tongue unleashes and snakes around her front, slipping into her parted mouth. I hear her gasp of surprise but it is soon swallowed up by her moans as my tongue fucks her throat in time with my cocks. Working in tandem to dominate every hole she has. Over and over again my hips slam into her. The globes of her ass cushion each blow. The wet suck of her pussy grips me and pulls me deeper inside her.

Irys is so wet that her arousal is dripping down my cock and slapping back against her ass. Messy. Just the way I like her. Her cunt begins to tighten around me and I know she's close.

Slipping my tongue from her mouth, her moans are even louder. She is delirious with pleasure. My tongue snakes back and dances over her clit and it is all over for her. Both her ass and pussy grip my cocks and I come the hardest I ever have.

I pitch forward and grip her hips, my claws digging in hard enough that I know I broke her skin. She screams as I shutter, filling both holes with rope after rope of my seed. Pulling out of her I watch it spray back out onto me and the sheets below. It runs down both of her openings in a continuous leak, coating the inside of both her thighs.

Absolutely perfect.

My magic zips again and my regular form has returned. I use my tongue to lick up the blood on her hips, my claws left behind and that has my cock hardening again. But my little Irys needs a break. Using one finger I sever the ribbon binding her arms and pull her up against my chest. Using my hands to rub the feeling back into her arm.

"That was incredible," she slurs, still floating on her orgasmic high.

"I'm glad you enjoyed that. I had been saving it for a special occasion but now felt special enough."

"Every time with you is special," Irys says, turning to press a kiss to my lips. Her arms circle around my neck and her legs wrap around my waist. A yawn sneaks up on her and I stand while she still clings to me. I turn to make my way to the bathroom but she squeezes my waist to make me stop.

"Fuck me again."

I laugh in surprise. "Irys, you're exhausted, I'll be inside you again soon enough. Let me clean you up and you can rest."

"I don't want to sleep. I want to come again."

"Greedy little slut," I say and kiss her brow. "But you're my greedy little slut. The only one who's privilege it is to serve this cunt."

"Only you, you'll own me forever." I grip her ass in my claws and notch my cock at her entrance. We will go slow this time and then I will put her to bed so she can be rested for another round tonight.

"Wrap your arms tighter around my neck." She does so immediately.

"Now be a good little girl and let me fuck you against the wall."

I would not be surprised if every creature who calls *The Woods* home could hear her scream.

The End

ACKNOWLEDGMENTS

Firstly, I want to say thank you to all of my readers. You all have blown me away with your support of my debut novel, *Taken by the Dark Elf King*. I am so grateful I do not have the words to express it. I am hoping this novella did it for me.

One thing I really wanted to work on were my spice scenes. As a new romance author, I wanted an opportunity to play with different tropes and kinks and see how I could make them into my own. Additionally, I am OBSESSED with Jessa Kane novellas and wanted to try out my own smutty short. I hope this novella tickled you in some way.

It was so much fun to write and I cannot wait for all of you to read the next one.

The monster romance community is one of the best in the whole world.

Until next time...xoxo Charlotte.

ABOUT THE AUTHOR

Charlotte Swan is twenty-four year old, living in Chicago. When she is not dreaming about being whisked away to a world filled with magic and sexy monsters, she is busy being a freelance social media marketer and full-time smut lover. To read her debut novel *Taken by the Dark Elf King*, hear about her upcoming projects, or to connect with her on social media please click the link below!

https://linktr.ee/authorcharlotteswan

ALSO BY CHARLOTTE SWAN

Kiss From a Monster Series

A Kiss From a Kraken (Kiss From a Monster Series Book 2)

Melody Rivers would give anything to go back to the way things were. Before her father had bartered away the last of her late mother's possessions to become a wealthy fisherman. One absorbed with his own selfish wants he barely has time for Melody anymore.

But her father's exploits on the high seas have not gone unnoticed...

The Kraken of the Darksea arrives to seek payment for her father's theft of his fish. What he decides to take instead is Melody.

Entranced by her beauty, the kraken will have her serve him in his bed chambers in his drowned palace for eternity.

Melody should be repulsed by this foul creature. However, she soon begins to realize he excites her more than he scares her. After saving her from a watery death Melody realizes that there's more to this beast than meets the eye. Will Melody give into his passion surfacing between them or let it drown in these dark waters of the sea?

Coming January 2023! Pre-Order today!

Monstrous Mates Series

Taken by the Dark Elf King: Monstrous Mates Series Book 1

Princess Elveena has never seen a dark elf in her life.

As princess of the light of elves, their two kinds have been separated since before her birth. When a royal messenger arrives inviting them to a ball hosted by the king of the dark elves, Elvie knows she cannot pass up on this once in a lifetime opportunity.

Even after the warnings from her father, Elvie knows this will be a night she'll never forget.

She expected to end the night with sore feet from the endless hours of dancing...*not to be engaged to the king himself!*

Trapped in this new kingdom, Elvie knows she must make the most of her new situation. With each passing day she learns that King Arkain is not what she thought a dark elf would be like. Sure he is mean and beastly compared to the males she is used to but, Elvie quickly finds that to be the reason he excites her so much.

As the threat of war looms, will this budding passion between Elvie and the king continue to blossom? Or will she lose herself and all that she loves in the process?

Captured by the Orc General: Monstrous Mates Book Two

Coming March 2023!

Royal alchemist Kaethe knows two things:

1 Drinking tea made from steeped riverhearts will cure almost anything.

2 Never, ever trust an orc.

But when a rumor, that she believes pertains to her missing brother, has her leaving the safety and warmth of King Arkain and Queen Elvie's court she finds herself in the heart of the orc's territory. Brokenbone Mountain is rumored to be filled with unspeakable danger. And if you are able to survive the harsh elements, those foul creatures that call the mountain home will enjoy feasting on your bones.

Delightful.

Bazur, General of the Black Claw Clan, has no time for humans. The years have turned him as cold as the mountain he calls home. The last thing he needs turning up in one of his traps is a brightly-colored hair human, who danger seems to be following like a shadow. Bazur should turn her away and let the beasts have an easy dinner. But there is something about her that stops him. That propels him to take her in and to keep her safe.

Even if she seems terrified of him.

When one of his clan-mates falls ill, Kaethe is the only one able to save him. In return, Bazur promises her safe passage through the mountain and he will act as her overseer while she sets about finding her brother.

As the nights on Brokenbone mountain grow longer and colder, both Kaethe and Bazur discover new things about each other. Will the distrust they harbor for each others kind give way to the passion brewing between them? Or will forces beyond their control separate them before they get the chance?